Dolphin
School

Flip's
Surprise Talent

Dolphin School

Flip's Surprise Talent

by Catherine Hapka
illustrated by Hollie Hibbert

SCHOLASTIC INC.

Text copyright © 2015 by Catherine Hapka
Illustrations copyright © 2015 by Scholastic Inc.

ISBN 978-0-545-75027-1

10 9 8 7 6 5 4 3 2 1   15 16 17 18 19/0

Printed in the U.S.A.   40
First printing, September 2015
Book design by Jennifer Rinaldi Windau

1

Big News

"Pearl! We're over here!"

Pearl was surprised to hear her friend Echo calling her. She was even more surprised when she saw that their other friends, Flip and Splash, were with her. The three of them were just inside the entrance of Coral Cove Dolphin School, floating in a patch of sunlight filtering down from the surface.

She swam toward them. "Good morning," she said. "I can't believe you're all here already! I thought I'd be the first one to get to school today." She smiled and flicked her fluke. "My little sister, Squeak, woke me up extra early."

Echo laughed. "Flip and I were ready to go early today, too."

Echo and Flip were members of the same pod—a dolphin family. Some pods were quite small, like Pearl's. She lived in a quiet lagoon with only her mother, father, and little sister. Other pods were much larger. There were more than fifty dolphins in Echo and Flip's pod. Pearl couldn't imagine living with that many other dolphins!

"These two even beat me here today!" Splash put in, doing a flip in the water.

Pearl smiled. Splash was the fastest swimmer she knew. He was almost always one of the first students to arrive at school.

"It's nice to get here early sometimes," Echo

said. "It's interesting to see what the reef is like without so many dolphins around."

Pearl nodded and glanced around the school. It was protected by a colorful coral reef that reached all the way up through the shallow waters of the cove and into the air above. The reef was home to lots of different kinds of sea creatures, from fish to mollusks to jellyfish. Right now a school of needlefish was zipping through the middle of the cove. On the sand below, a blue crab scuttled along, dodging around a cluster of oysters.

"This place is great, isn't it?" Pearl blew a happy stream of bubbles from her blowhole. "I wonder what we're going to do in Magic class today. I hope we practice more healing skills—that was interesting yesterday."

Young dolphins from all over this part of the Salty Sea came to Coral Cove Dolphin School to learn everything they needed to know, including how to use their natural magical abilities. Pearl and her friends were all in their first year there.

Splash laughed. "Why are you thinking about Magic already?" he said. "That class isn't until the end of the day. Shouldn't you be wondering about Music class instead? That comes first. Besides, you're awesome at music, Pearl!"

"She's good at magic, too," Echo said. "When she healed that broken piece of coral in class, it looked as good as new."

Pearl smiled. "Thanks. I know I'm not as good at magic as you are, though."

"Nobody's as good at magic as Echo," Flip said. "Except maybe her mom!"

Pearl nodded. Echo's mother had extra strong magic. She was famous throughout the Salty Sea for rescuing some Land Leggers when their boat sank. Dolphins were the protectors of the ocean, and that meant they were always willing to help all the creatures who lived under the waves—or over them. Pearl was sure that one day Echo would be just as good at magic as her mother was.

"But nobody's as good at Music as Pearl," Splash said. "Anyway, I'm glad that Music and Magic aren't our only classes. Otherwise they'd probably kick me out of school!"

Echo smiled. "Don't worry, Splash," she said. "Everyone knows you're the best at Jumping and Swimming."

"Or at least he's tied for best," Flip said, doing a flip just like the one Splash had done. "I'm just as good as he is."

Pearl shared a smile with Echo. Flip bragged a lot about almost everything. At first that had bothered Pearl, but it didn't bother her anymore. She liked everything about her friends.

"That's one of the best things about school," Splash said. "There are enough different classes so that everyone is good at something."

"Except Ocean Lore, maybe," Echo said with a giggle. "Nobody's good at listening to Old Salty's boring lectures on algae and barnacles!"

Pearl giggled, too. But she also looked around to make sure Old Salty wasn't nearby. She didn't want to hurt his feelings—even if his lectures were a little dull.

She didn't see the Ocean Lore teacher anywhere. Instead, she spotted two other students swimming into the school.

Echo spotted them, too. "Uh oh," she whispered. "Here comes Mullet."

Mullet was a year ahead of them in school. He was friends with Splash's brother. But that didn't mean he was nice to Splash or the other younger dolphins. In fact, he liked to bully the younger kids every chance he got.

"I don't know why Shelly hangs out with Mullet," Pearl whispered, glancing at the dolphin swimming beside Mullet. "She seems really nice."

By then the older dolphins had reached them. "What are you babies doing here so early?" Mullet asked with a smirk. "Never mind, I know why. You're such nerds that you probably wish you could stay at school all the time."

"No, we don't," Flip shot back.

"We do love school, though," Echo added. "What's wrong with that?"

"Nothing," Shelly spoke up with a smile. "I like school, too."

"Yeah, but you're not a nerd like them," Mullet said.

Shelly laughed. "Oh, Mullet! You're so silly!"

Pearl traded a look with her friends. Shelly never seemed to notice when Mullet was being mean.

Shelly was still smiling at them. "Anyway, I don't blame you for wanting to get here early," she said. "I can tell you're all really good friends. Very compatible."

"Compatible?" Splash said. "What does that mean?"

"It means we belong together, like fins and water," Echo told him.

"More like algae and slime," Mullet muttered as he swam off.

"Bye, you guys!" Shelly sang out, swimming after him.

"Mullet is so mean," Flip said with a frown.

"Never mind him." Echo blew out a stream of bubbles. "Let's talk about something more fun—like all the cool stuff we'll be doing in school today!"

And so they did. They were still talking a few minutes later when Old Salty swam to the middle of the cove and called for attention. Most of the other students and teachers had arrived by then.

"I have good news," Old Salty said once everyone was listening. "It's time for the school's annual Show Off Day!"

2

Show Off Day
Is Coming!

"Show Off Day?" Flip exclaimed. "Wow, that's awesome!"

"Yeah!" Splash did three flips in a row. "I can't believe it's here already—I can't wait!"

Echo laughed. "This is the best day ever!"

Pearl looked around. Everyone else seemed just as excited as her friends. They were chattering and doing flips and blowing bubbles. Old Salty just watched and smiled.

"Show Off Day?" Pearl said to her friends. "What's that?"

"Are you joking?" Flip said. "Everyone knows what Show Off Day is."

"I don't," Pearl said.

"It's when all the students at Coral Cove Dolphin School get to show off what they've learned so far that year," Echo explained. "The whole dolphin community comes to watch. Didn't you ever go with your pod?"

Splash nodded. "I thought everyone went."

One of the teachers swam over. Her name was Bay, and she taught Pearl's two favorite classes, Magic and Music.

"I heard what you were saying," she told the young dolphins. "There's a good reason why Pearl hasn't been to Show Off Day before. As you all know, her pod has a very important job protecting baby sea turtles."

Pearl nodded. Lots of turtles laid their eggs on the island by her pod's lagoon. The dolphins helped guide the hatchlings out to sea, where they would be safe from hungry gulls and other land predators.

"Yeah, we know all about that," Flip said. "What do a bunch of baby turtles have to do with Show Off Day?"

"Normally Show Off Day happens around the same time of year that the turtles hatch," Bay explained. "That's why Pearl's pod never came before. They didn't want to leave their lagoon during that very important time."

"Oh." Pearl was worried. "Does that mean I'll have to miss Show Off Day this year, too?"

Bay smiled. "No, you'll be there, and so

will your pod," she assured Pearl. "We made it earlier this year so you won't have to miss it."

"Really?" Echo bumped Pearl's side with her snout. "That's super, Pearl!"

"Yeah," Splash said. "Show Off Day wouldn't be the same without you."

Flip nodded. "It's great! Everyone talks about the best performances all year afterward. This year, one of those best performances is going to be me!"

Bay chuckled. "All we ask is that you do your best, Flip. And have fun, of course."

Pearl smiled at Bay. "Thanks for telling me about Show Off Day," she said. "Now I can't wait to be a part of it."

Just then Old Salty called for attention again. "I'm glad you're all so excited," he told all the students with a chuckle. "We'll have our regular classes today as usual. But tomorrow you'll have the whole day to figure out your routines and get started on practicing. Show Off Day will be two days after that."

"That's right." Bay swam forward to join him. "As always, group performances are encouraged. Remember that dolphins are at their best when they work together."

Pearl looked at her friends. "Group performances?"

"Yeah!" Splash did a flip. "Let's work together, okay?"

"Sure," Echo said. "We make a good group."

Flip zipped up to get a breath of air, then swam back down. "So what kind of performance should we do?" he asked. "Whatever it is, it has to be great—I want our group to be the best!"

"We will be," Pearl said with a smile. "Because we're compatible. That's what Shelly said, remember?"

Echo didn't seem to be listening. She was staring off into the distance with a thoughtful expression.

"Echo?" Pearl said. "What are you thinking about?"

Echo smiled and sent out a burst of sparkly magic lights. "I was just thinking about how we could do a super amazing magic display," she said eagerly. "I already have some ideas for really fancy stuff we could do."

"A magic display?" Splash sounded dubious. "Everyone will be doing that kind of thing. I think we should do a cool jumping and swimming routine instead."

Pearl didn't like the sound of that. She wasn't very good at jumping and swimming. This would be her first Show Off Day ever, and she wanted their performance to be something she could do well. Something like magic, or . . .

"What about singing a song?" she blurted

out, realizing it was the perfect idea. "We've been learning some neat things in Music class."

Flip looked over as Old Salty called out for everyone to swim to their first classes. "Like I said, I don't care what we do," he said. "I'm great at everything. And I can't wait to show it off!"

That made the other three laugh. "Let's get together after school," Pearl suggested as the four of them swam toward Music class. "We can figure out what to do then."

3

An Important Decision

AFTER SCHOOL, PEARL AND HER FRIENDS gathered in a sunny spot outside the reef. "I'm not sure the water is deep enough here for some of the tricks I want us to try," Splash said, looking around. "We don't want to bump our snouts on the sand."

"Hang on," Echo said. "We didn't agree to do your idea. I still think we should do some really cool magic instead."

"That would be okay," Pearl said. "But did any of you think about my idea? With all four of us singing, we could perform a really nice song that everyone would like."

"That's true," Flip said. "I'm great at singing. But I'm great at the other stuff, too. Which idea do you guys think will impress everyone the most?"

"Definitely magic," Echo replied right away.

"No way! My idea would be much more interesting," Splash said.

"Everyone loves a good dolphin song," Pearl put in. She hoped she could convince her friends to go along with her idea. She was excited about the chance to show her parents what she'd learned in school so far. Echo's magic idea could be fun, but Pearl was better at music. With everybody watching, she wanted to do the thing she could do the best.

"We need to figure out a plan soon." Flip sounded a little impatient. "We don't have much time to practice, and I want us to be amazing."

Mullet swam past just in time to hear him. "Amazing?" he said in a mean voice. "The only amazing thing is that first years are allowed to be in Show Off Day at all. Nobody is going to pay any attention to your baby display. You don't even know anything yet."

"Yes, we do, and yes, they will," Flip retorted. "We're going to be great! Right, guys?"

"Definitely," Echo agreed. "Our magic

display will be like nothing anybody's ever done at Show Off Day before."

"You mean our jumping and swimming routine," Splash corrected.

"Didn't you hear what I said about doing a group song?" Pearl put in. "I know it would be really good."

Mullet looked around at all of them. "Wow, it sounds like you can't even decide what to do. You'd better figure something out soon, or you'll look silly in front of the entire dolphin community."

"We're deciding right now," Flip told him. "You don't have to worry about us looking silly."

"Oh, I'm not worried. I *know* you're going to look silly." Mullet smirked. "But don't be too upset. Nobody will even remember your performance once they see my group."

"Really?" Pearl couldn't help being curious. "What are you guys doing?"

"Shelly's already working on our song, and it's going to be the best," Mullet bragged. "Finny and I are great singers. We're almost as good as Shelly, and everyone knows she's the best in the whole school."

Pearl felt nervous. Shelly was super talented at both music and magic—everyone did know that. Could her own ideas for a musical performance ever measure up to Shelly's song?

"Songs are boring," Splash declared. "Our jumping and swimming display will be much more exciting."

"You mean our amazing magic performance," Echo put in.

"Whatever." Mullet rolled his eyes. "Like

I said, you'd better hurry up and decide what you're doing. Otherwise Old Salty might not let you be in the show at all!"

He swam off with a swirl of bubbles. Pearl glanced at her friends, worried.

"Is that true?" she asked. "If we don't decide what we're doing right away, will we be banned from performing?" Now that she knew about Show Off Day, it was terrible to think about something like that happening! She was already looking forward to showing her pod how well she was doing in school.

"No, Mullet's just trying to get our fins in a flurry," Echo assured her. "Everyone gets to participate, no matter what."

"Yeah." Splash grinned. "Remember two years ago? Those girls messed up their magic show because they didn't bother to practice."

"You mean the ones who accidentally sent all those pinching crabs into the audience instead of making them dance?" Flip said with a laugh. "I remember that."

"So do I. Everyone was talking about it for ages afterward," Echo agreed with a shudder. "But not in a good way."

"Don't worry, that won't be us," Flip said. "But Mullet is right about one thing. We need to decide what we're doing soon so we have plenty of time to practice."

"What do you think about my idea to do a song?" Pearl said quickly, before her friends could respond. "I know it would be really good."

"Not as good as my magic idea." Echo sent out a burst of magical sparkles that floated up through the water.

"I keep telling you, we should do jumping and swimming," Splash said. "Why aren't you guys listening?"

"Why aren't you listening to me?" Echo retorted. "You're not even giving my idea a chance!"

"Neither are you," Pearl blurted out. "Everyone knows you're great at magic, but what about the rest of us? We need something we can all do well!"

"Like jumping and swimming," Splash put in, doing a quick flip.

Pearl sent out a frustrated burst of bubbles. "No, not like that," she said. "You know I'm not very good in Jumping and Swimming class. Why would I want to show that off to everyone?"

"Well, why would I want to show everyone

that I can barely do enough magic to convince a fish to swim?" Splash retorted. "Jumping and swimming is what I do best, and that's what I want to do."

"Come on, you guys," Flip put in. "We'll never impress anyone on Show Off Day if we can't even agree on what to do!"

"Well, what do *you* want to do?" Echo asked him. "We have one vote each for our three ideas. That means you get the deciding vote." She touched his fin and smiled. "And everyone knows you're great at magic. You might even be a little better than me."

"Hey!" Splash protested. "You don't really think that. You're trying to convince him to vote with you."

"How do you know she doesn't mean it?" Flip sounded a little hurt. "I am great at magic."

"You're a good singer, too," Pearl reminded him. "Don't you want to do music for the show?"

"Sure, I guess that would be okay," Flip said.

"No!" Splash exclaimed. "Lots of dolphins do songs. And even more do magic. We should do something different—like this cool new flip I made up the other day . . ."

"Aargh!" Echo exclaimed. "You're hopeless, Splash."

"What do you mean? I'm just saying what I think," Splash said.

"Well, I'm saying what I think is best for *all* of us," Echo shot back.

"No, you're not!" Pearl blurted out without thinking. "You're both just being as stubborn as a squid!"

Echo looked slightly hurt. "Am not," she said. "Anyway, you're being stubborn, too, Pearl."

"Yeah," Splash said.

Pearl didn't know what to say. She'd never argued with her friends like this, and she didn't like it one bit.

"I—I have to go home," she blurted out.

"Fine." Echo sounded annoyed. "We'll decide what to do tomorrow."

4

Flip's Idea

THE NEXT MORNING, PEARL SWAM SLOWLY toward the school reef. For once, she wasn't very eager to get there. She was still upset about yesterday's argument. What if Echo, Splash, and Flip didn't want to be friends with her anymore because she'd disagreed with them and called them stubborn? Not being friends anymore was the worst thing she could imagine.

"Show Off Day sounded like fun at first," she mumbled to herself. "But now I wish I'd never heard of it!"

She swam into the reef and looked around. She didn't see Echo or Splash. But Flip was floating near some feathery sea plumes that were growing out of the reef.

When he spotted Pearl, he swam over. "I was waiting for you," he said. He sounded worried. "I need to talk to you."

Pearl was glad that he still wanted to talk to her. Then again, Flip hadn't seemed as mad as the other two yesterday. He hadn't seemed to care which idea they did. Not like Echo and Splash, who had been so stubborn about only wanting to do their own ideas for Show Off Day.

Maybe I was a little bit stubborn, too, like they said, Pearl reminded herself, feeling guilty. *I didn't want to listen to their ideas, either.*

"Okay," she said to Flip. "What do you want to talk about?"

Flip looked around. "Come over here where nobody will hear us," he said.

He led the way to a quiet nook behind some large growths of stony coral. Then he turned to face Pearl, looking much more serious than usual.

"I wish we hadn't gotten into that argument yesterday," he said. "We're supposed to be working as a group. But nobody was even listening to anyone else."

Pearl nodded. "I know," she said. "But what are we supposed to do about it? Our ideas were all so different."

"You're good at helping people get along," Flip said. "And we're all friends, right?"

"Right," Pearl said, hoping that was still true.

"That means we should be able to agree

on a plan," Flip went on. "You should talk to Splash and Echo. Maybe you can convince them to try again." He blew out a small burst of bubbles. "Because we really need to figure out what to do, or we'll look silly on Show Off Day! Just like Mullet said."

"Okay, I'll try," Pearl said. "I just hope they listen to me this time."

The two of them swam out from behind the stony coral. Pearl saw Splash swimming in through the entrance. She also spotted Echo floating nearby, talking to a couple of the other dolphins from their school pod.

Flip rushed off to get Splash, while Pearl swam over to Echo. "Can we talk for a second?" she asked.

"Sure." Echo said good-bye to the other dolphins, then followed Pearl back toward the two boys. "I was just talking to Harmony. She and the other three from our pod are already practicing a jumping and swimming routine. It sounds like they're going to be really good."

Flip heard her. "Really?" he said. "Yeah, Wiggle and Harmony are both great at fancy flips and stuff. But I know we could do an even better performance, if . . ." He trailed off and looked at Pearl.

Pearl blew out some bubbles, feeling nervous. "Look, you guys," she blurted out. "Your friendship means more to me than some stupid Show Off Day routine. I'm sorry I was so stubborn yesterday."

"Me too," Echo said immediately, touching her fin to Pearl's. "I'm sorry I wouldn't listen."

Splash looked sheepish. "Me three. I don't want to fight with you guys."

"Good." Flip sounded relieved. "See? We still make a great team. That's why we're going to be the best at Show Off Day."

Pearl was relieved, too. She never wanted to fight with her friends again!

She looked around at the others, waiting for them to offer to do her music idea. But Echo and Splash just stared back at her.

"Um, so how are we going to figure out what to do?" Pearl asked at last.

Flip looked uncertain for a moment. Then he brightened.

"I know," he exclaimed. "A bubble burst!"

"A what?" Splash asked.

But Echo smiled. "It's something we do in our pod sometimes," she explained. "It's a way of leaving decisions up to chance."

Flip nodded. "How it works is, the three

of you each blow one big air bubble." To demonstrate, he sent a single bubble floating up out of his blowhole. "Then we see whose bubble lasts the longest before popping."

"Whoever has the last bubble wins," Echo finished. "And we'll do that dolphin's idea for the show."

Pearl wasn't sure what to think. If Splash won the bubble burst, she would have to do jumping and swimming, and she still wasn't sure she wanted to do that. But she supposed it was the only fair way to decide.

"Okay," she said. "Anything's better than more arguing."

"Definitely," Splash said. "Let's do it!"

They all swam up to the surface. Pearl took in a deep gulp of air, floating there for a moment watching some seagulls swoop and circle overhead. Then she dove down with the others.

"Okay, on the count of three," Flip said. "One . . . two . . . three . . . blow!"

Pearl, Echo, and Splash each blew a big air bubble. Pearl held her breath as she watched hers float slowly upward. It was larger than Echo's, but not quite as big as Splash's.

"Oh no!" Splash cried as his bubble popped and disappeared into the current.

Pearl was relieved. At least that meant she wouldn't have to do jumping and swimming for the show!

A second later her own bubble burst. "Oh!" she exclaimed, disappointed.

"Yay!" Echo cried at the same time. "I win! We're doing magic!"

5

Echo's Magical Plans

PEARL WAS STILL A LITTLE DISAPPOINTED that she hadn't won the bubble burst. But she liked magic just as much as music, even if she wasn't quite as good at it. Besides, Echo was so good at magic that her plan for the show was probably great.

"What's your idea?" she asked Echo.

Echo looked excited. "I haven't worked out all the details yet," she said. "But I was thinking we could start by guiding a school of pretty fish in to hide us from the audience. Then we'll guide them to swim off in all directions, so everyone will suddenly see us floating there behind them."

"I get it." Flip nodded. "That sounds really cool!"

Pearl agreed. Guiding was a magical skill that all the dolphins had been practicing since the first day of class. It involved magically asking other sea creatures to do something. Most fish and crustaceans were usually willing to be guided by dolphins, although some other types of creatures could be more stubborn. Guiding large schools of fish was harder than guiding one or a few, but Echo's magic was very strong. With all four of them working together, Pearl was pretty sure they could do what Echo had in mind.

"I bet everyone will love that," she said.

"Yeah." Echo swam around in a circle. "But

that's definitely not all! After the fish reveal us there, that's when the show really starts!"

"What do you mean?" Splash asked.

"I want to show off all our magical skills," Echo said. "So next we'll call in a few snapping shrimp."

"Isn't that using the same skill?" Flip asked. "I mean, we'll call the shrimp using guiding, won't we?"

"Yes, but I'm not finished," Echo said. "Snapping shrimp make lots of noise, right?"

Pearl nodded. There were plenty of snapping shrimp near her home lagoon. They had a special claw that they could use to create a loud snapping sound. Sometimes the noise was so loud that it woke her up at night!

"We'll guide the shrimp to snap, and then use our physical magic to make the sounds louder and softer."

"Like music?" Pearl said.

Echo shrugged. "Sort of, I guess. But it will mostly be a way to show off how well we can use our magic."

"Okay," Splash said uncertainly. "But we only started practicing that stuff recently. Do you think we can do it?"

"Sure we can," Flip told him. "It's not that hard. Plus Echo is super at all kinds of magic."

"And then after that," Echo went on, "I was thinking we could bring in some fish and crabs and stuff, and guide them all to dance while we create a really cool light display with a rainbow over it all."

"What?" Pearl blurted out. "Light displays and rainbows? But we haven't done any of that stuff in class yet!"

"It's okay, my mom taught me," Echo said with a wave of her fin. "I can show you guys how to do it."

Pearl traded a worried look with Splash. Did Echo remember that they weren't as talented at magic as she was? They hadn't grown up with super-talented magical mothers, either.

"Maybe we should skip the last part," Pearl suggested. "We could still do the other stuff."

"Maybe," Splash added dubiously.

Echo frowned. "But it won't be as special without the light display," she said. "It'll be fine—you'll see."

Just then Old Salty called the school to attention, so Pearl and the others stopped talking.

"All right, everyone," Old Salty said with a smile. "I know we're all excited to see what you students come up with for this year's Show Off Day. You'll have all of today and tomorrow to work on your performances. Please feel free to consult any of us teachers if you need help. Now let's get started!"

Most of the students cheered, including Echo and Flip. But Pearl and Splash stayed quiet.

"Do you think we can do everything Echo has planned?" Pearl asked Splash in a low voice.

"I don't know about you, but I'm pretty sure I can't," Splash responded, with a burst of bubbles. "I have trouble just guiding one or two fish, never mind all that other stuff."

"Stop whispering over there, you two," Echo said cheerfully. "It's time to get started."

"Okay," Splash said. "But maybe we should talk about your ideas. It might be better to do a less complicated routine."

"I agree," Pearl said. "It's better to stick to magic we know we can do well. Maybe we could just guide the fish and shrimp like you said, and then maybe do some mental messaging to the audience or something?"

Echo shook her head. "Anybody can do that stuff," she said. "We want our display to be extra special."

"Yeah!" Flip sounded excited. "We want to be the best!"

Pearl knew that Flip wanted to do well at Show Off Day. And she guessed that Echo wanted to impress her mother and the rest of her pod with her magic skills. But what if they couldn't do all that complicated magic properly? Instead of impressing everyone, they could embarrass themselves in front of the whole dolphin community!

She wanted to say that to Echo. But she was afraid she'd get mad.

Besides, Mom and Dad always say to try my best, Pearl reminded herself. *I'll just do that—and hope it works.*

They got started, practicing guiding a school of fish a few times. Everyone was pretty good at that, even though Splash kept getting distracted and letting his part of the school wander off in the wrong direction.

Finally Echo seemed satisfied. "Okay," she said. "I haven't seen any snapping shrimp around today, so let's practice the light display next. Pearl and Flip, join your magic and try to guide some cool-looking fish over here. I'll work with Splash on the light display."

Pearl touched her fin to Flip's. "I'm not sure we can do this," she said, feeling nervous.

"Sure we can." He sounded confident. "Guiding fish is easy."

"That's not what I meant," Pearl murmured.

But Flip wasn't listening. He was already sending out waves of magical energy toward some pretty blue parrot fish floating nearby. Pearl joined her magic with his, guiding the fish closer.

Nearby, she saw magical lights and sparkles start to form in the water by Echo and Splash. "More," Echo urged. "Focus your magic, Splash!"

"I'm trying!" Splash sounded frazzled. "But I told you, I don't know how to do this stuff!"

"Just do what I said!" Echo exclaimed.

Pearl's eyes widened as a rainbow started to form in the water over their heads. She was so distracted that she forgot about the parrot fish.

"Pearl, you have to help me," Flip exclaimed. "They're swimming away!"

"Oops." Pearl spun around, sending out another burst of magical energy. But she was still distracted by the rainbow, too. She turned to look at it—and accidentally sent her magic toward Splash instead of the fish.

"Hey!" he shouted in surprise as the energy hit him, sending his own magical energy bouncing off in the wrong direction.

"Oh no!" Echo cried as a bunch of bright, spinning magical sparkles shot wildly across the cove—right into Bay's face!

The teacher looked surprised. She swam toward the group.

"What's going on over here?" she asked.

"Sorry, Bay," Pearl said. "Our magic got a little out of control. We didn't mean to do that."

"I see." Luckily, Bay didn't sound mad. "What are you four working on?"

Echo quickly told Bay about her plans. When she finished, Bay looked concerned.

"That's a lot of pretty advanced magic for first-year students," she said. "I'm not sure it's a good idea to use skills we haven't practiced in class yet. I think perhaps you should skip the light display and rainbow."

"I guess you're right." Echo sounded sheepish. "Thanks, Bay."

Bay nodded and swam off. Pearl was

relieved, but she could see that Echo was disappointed.

"It'll be okay," she said, touching Echo's fin. "Our show will still be good even without the light display."

"No, it won't," Echo said with a sigh. "Just doing guiding and basic sound stuff won't impress anyone at all!" She shrugged. "Maybe we shouldn't do magic after all."

"You mean you want to do one of the other ideas?" Splash said.

"Maybe we should," Flip said. "Without the light stuff, the magic display would be boring." He pointed a fin at Pearl. "You came in second in the bubble burst. Pearl. Let's do your idea."

6

A Musical Mess

AT FIRST PEARL WASN'T SURE WHAT TO THINK or say. "Oh," she said. "Um . . ."

"Hurry up and tell us more about your idea," Flip urged. "We've already lost tons of time. We'll need to make up for it so we're still one of the best groups."

"O-okay," Pearl stammered. She did her best to focus, trying to remember all the great ideas for songs that she'd had the day before. "I guess I was thinking we could combine all our special dolphin songs into one big song?"

On the first day of school, Bay had reminded

the Music class that each adult dolphin had a unique dolphin song. Part of what she was doing in class was helping each young dolphin start to develop his or her own special song.

"That's a great idea, Pearl," Flip said. "I'm sure it will impress Bay—and everyone else, too!"

"Good." Pearl smiled with relief. "Then maybe we should start out by each doing a short solo of part of our song. Then we can create different harmonies by combining the songs together, first in pairs, and then all four of us."

Splash did a flip, looking nervous. "That sounds complicated."

"Don't worry." Pearl gave him a reassuring fin rub. "I'll help you."

"Okay, you start, Pearl," Flip suggested.

"Then I'll do my solo after yours."

Pearl nodded. Swimming up to the surface, she took a deep breath. Then she returned to her friends and started to sing.

Pearl had been working hard on her special song. She was proud of it, and glad that she'd get to show it off to her pod and everyone else.

When she finished her part, Flip sang his solo. It sounded good.

Next it was Echo's turn, and she started to sing. Her voice was never quite as strong as Pearl's, but usually it was pretty nice. Today, however, it sounded weak and a little shaky. Pearl was confused—until she noticed little bursts of magical sparkles floating around her friend.

"Hey," she said. "What are you doing, Echo?"

Echo stopped singing. "What do you mean?"

"Those sparkles." Flip swished his tail to send the last of the pretty lights floating off on the current. "We're supposed to be doing music, remember? Not magic."

Echo shrugged. "I just thought a light display might make the performance more interesting."

"Well, it's making your song sound bad," Flip told her. "That makes us all look bad."

"Why don't you try again, without the magic?" Pearl suggested.

"Fine." Echo looked annoyed. She swam up for air, then started her song again.

When she finished, it was Splash's turn. His song was loud, but not very good. He kept messing up the melody, and getting faster and faster.

"Maybe you should sing a shorter part of your song, Splash," Pearl suggested when he finished.

"Yeah, you're right," Splash said with a laugh. "How about this?"

He started again, singing a shorter part. But it sounded just as bad. Pearl winced. What would everyone think if Splash's terrible song was part of their performance?

"Maybe we should go right from Echo's song into a duet between her and Splash," she blurted.

"What?" Flip sounded surprised. "You can't leave out Splash's part. This is supposed to be a group project. What will everyone think if he's the only one who doesn't have a solo at the beginning?"

Pearl knew he was right. But how could she help Splash improve in just a couple of days?

Before she could figure it out, she saw Splash's brother, Finny, swimming toward them. "How's it going?" he asked. "What are you guys doing for your performance?"

"Music," Splash told him with a sigh.

"Yeah," Pearl muttered. "At least we're *trying* to do music."

Finny shrugged. "We're doing music, too."

"We know," Flip said. "Mullet told us Shelly's been working on your song."

"She already finished it." Finny sounded excited. "It's really great! It's different from any Show Off Day song we've ever heard before. Everyone is going to love it!"

"Really?" Flip sounded wistful.

Pearl wondered if Flip wished he could join Finny's group instead of theirs. She was starting to wish the same thing herself!

No, I'm not, she told herself as Finny swam away. *I want to work with my friends. I just wish I was as talented as Shelly. Maybe then I could figure out how to fix our performance . . .*

"I don't think we should do music after all," she said suddenly.

"What?" Flip sounded surprised. "What do you mean, Pearl?"

She blew out a nervous stream of bubbles. "I just don't know if we can practice enough to sound really good," she said. "We should probably do something else instead."

She glanced at Echo, expecting her to take over again with her magic idea. Instead, Splash did four quick flips and a spin.

"Great!" he shouted. "I came in third in the bubble burst. That means we're doing jumping and swimming!"

7

Jumping, Swimming, Flipping, and Spinning

PEARL'S HEART SANK. JUMPING AND swimming? She was just as bad at that as Splash was at music. What if she looked silly in front of everyone because she couldn't keep up with her friends? What if she messed up so badly that she made her friends look silly, too?

But it was too late to back out now. Everyone

else was listening to Splash as he explained his ideas.

"First we'll all swim in really fast," he said, zipping back and forth in front of them to demonstrate. "Then we'll all do a roll at the same time."

He rolled over in the water as he swam. It made Pearl dizzy just watching!

"Cool!" Flip said. He did a roll, too. "Then what?"

"Let's practice that part first," Splash said. "I'm still thinking about what to do next. And we don't have much time to practice."

"Okay," Echo said. "Should we go in a line?"

"Yes." Splash swam over next to Flip. "Echo, get on my other side. Pearl, you go next to Flip."

Pearl did as he said. "Should we get more air first?" she asked. "I might need—"

"Go!" Splash shouted before she could finish.

He and Flip swam forward as fast as they could. That was pretty fast! Echo was a second late getting started, but she did her best to catch up.

"Wait!" Pearl cried. "I wasn't ready."

She swam after her friends. By the time she caught up, they'd all stopped.

"What happened?" Splash asked. "I said go."

"I know. I'm sorry." Pearl swam up to take a breath. "I was low on air."

"Oh. Okay, then let's try it again," Splash said. "Everybody line up!"

Pearl hurried to obey, just like she did when their Jumping and Swimming teacher, Riptide, barked out an order. In fact, Splash sounded a little like Riptide right now. Riptide was loud and impatient, and he never stopped moving. Splash never stopped moving, either. But he usually wasn't so loud or impatient.

"Pearl!" Splash snapped. "Are you paying attention? We have to get this part right before we can work on the rest of our routine."

"Yeah, pay attention," Flip urged. "I want

us to be really good, and that means we need a lot of practice."

"Sorry," Pearl said again. "I'm paying attention."

This time when Splash shouted go, Pearl started swimming at the same time as the others. She was a little behind as they all started their rolls, but she did her best.

"Hmm," Splash said when they finished. "Maybe we can come back to that part later. Let's move on to some flips and jumps."

Pearl gulped. "I'm not very good at those," she reminded Splash.

"You'll do fine." He waved a fin. "Follow me, everyone. We'll start by doing a triple flip underwater, and then swim up to the surface and do a forward jump, and then a backward flip in the air."

"That sounds pretty hard," Echo said. "Maybe we should do something easier between jumps."

"Easy stuff won't impress anyone," Flip said. "We should at least try it."

"Yeah, let's go!" Splash said. "Everyone follow me."

Without waiting for a response, he started his first underwater flip. Flip did the same, and so did Echo.

Pearl had never even done a single flip before starting school. She was getting much better at them. But she was still slower than her friends. By the time she finished her third flip, Splash was already zipping up toward the surface for his jumps.

Whew, Pearl thought. *I hope I survive until Show Off Day!*

They kept practicing for a long time without taking a break. After a while, everyone was exhausted. Well, everyone except Splash. He was still excited about his ideas.

"That last jump was better, Pearl," he said as the whole group finished another set of movements. "We can work on it more later. Because I just had an idea—we should do that tail walking thing Riptide showed us that time!"

"What?!" Pearl cried.

She remembered that day in Jumping and Swimming class. Riptide had demonstrated a fancy move where he lifted his whole body out of the water, with only his tail holding him upright. He'd had the whole class try, but only Splash and a few others had been able to do it pretty well. Pearl hadn't been able to do it at all!

"We can't do that." Echo shot Pearl a worried look. "Some of us aren't, um, very good at it."

"I can do it," Flip bragged. "Watch!"

He zoomed up and lifted himself out of the water. But he was moving too fast, and flopped down almost immediately, crashing into part of the coral wall.

"Ow," he said. "Oops."

Old Salty noticed the commotion and bustled over. "What are you doing?" he exclaimed. "Be careful, young fellow—you nearly dislodged those poor, innocent tube sponges!" He swam closer and peered at the bulbous purple and yellow shapes stuck to the coral wall.

"Sorry." Flip rubbed a scratch on his side with one fin.

"We were just practicing for Show Off Day," Splash added.

"Well, you need to be careful," Old Salty said. "The reef is very delicate, and you can't just go crashing into it willy-nilly!"

"We'll be more careful, we promise," Echo told him.

"All right, see that you do." Old Salty gave them one last stern look. Then he swam off.

8

Working Together?

"THIS ISN'T WORKING," ECHO SAID AS SOON as Old Salty was gone. "Splash, we just can't keep up with you when it comes to jumping and swimming!"

"I can," Flip said. "I was keeping up just fine."

"No, you weren't," Echo told him, flicking her tail toward the coral wall. "You just proved that by crashing into those sponges."

Splash glanced at Flip, then shrugged. "Maybe I can do the tail walking by myself, and you guys can do jumps next to me. I know! I could teach you that cool shark jump

I learned. That would look really cool."

"No!" Pearl cried. It came out louder than she planned, and all three of her friends turned to look at her.

"What?" Flip said.

Pearl blew out a stream of bubbles. "No," she said more quietly. "I don't want to learn to do that shark jump. I don't want to do jumping and swimming at all!"

"Why not?" Splash sounded surprised. "Jumping and swimming is fun!"

"It is for you, because you're good at it," Pearl told him. "It's not that much fun for me, especially with all the complicated stuff you want us to do." She was so upset that her snout quivered. "I don't want to look stupid in front of everyone on Show Off Day because I can't keep up."

"Well, now you know how I felt before," Splash said. "I couldn't keep up with my part in your song."

Pearl hadn't thought about it that way. Was singing just as hard and frustrating for Splash as jumping and swimming were for Pearl?

"Come on, you guys, we don't have time to argue." Flip sounded anxious. "Maybe we need to go back to the music idea."

Echo shrugged. "Maybe. Splash, I bet you could sing better if you practiced more."

"Or maybe we could do a simpler song," Flip suggested.

"I guess we could try," Pearl said. "Instead of all of us doing solos, just one or two of us could do them."

"Or we could skip the solos and just sing together," Splash said.

"No!" Pearl said. "It wouldn't be the same without any solos."

Flip flicked his tail from side to side, looking impatient. "If we can't agree, maybe we should go back to Echo's magic idea."

Echo brightened. "You want to try that again?" she said. "Maybe we could skip the rainbow and just do the light display."

"Or maybe we could skip the light display, too," Pearl said. "It's too hard. Even Bay said so."

Echo frowned. "But it wouldn't be the same without that part!"

"Hey, I never said I was giving up my turn to do jumping and swimming," Splash spoke up, doing an underwater backflip. "I guess we could leave out the tail walking if you guys really don't want to do it."

"Okay," Echo said. "But we'd have to leave

out the shark spin, too. And maybe some of the other jumps."

"What?" Splash exclaimed. "No way! It wouldn't be the same without that stuff!"

Flip blew out a frustrated burst of bubbles. "We can't float here arguing all day!" he cried. "We need to figure out what we're going to do. Otherwise we won't be ready to do anything!"

Pearl knew he was right. But how would they ever agree on what to do for their performance?

"I don't mind doing one of your ideas," she told Echo and Splash. "But not if you force me to embarrass myself by asking me to do more than I can. That's not fair."

"She's right," Flip agreed. "It won't really count as a group project if the whole group can't join in." He looked thoughtful. "Actually . . ."

"Actually," Echo broke in before Flip could continue, "I think you're right, Flip."

"I am?" Flip said.

"Yes." Echo nodded. "If we can't all agree on an idea, maybe we shouldn't be a group after all."

"What are you saying?" Pearl asked.

Echo shrugged. "I'm saying maybe we should each do our own thing for Show Off Day."

"You mean go solo?" Flip said.

"Sounds good to me," Splash spoke up. "Then I can do all the tail walking I want."

"Yeah," Echo said. "And I can do all the magic I want."

Pearl hesitated, trading a look with Flip. She didn't want to go solo. And she guessed that he didn't, either.

But Echo and Splash were already swimming off in opposite directions. "Oh well," Flip said. "I guess we're not a group anymore."

Then he swam away, too, leaving Pearl all alone.

9

Working Apart

PEARL COULDN'T BELIEVE IT. DID HER FRIENDS really care more about impressing everyone at Show Off Day than they did about working together? Shelly had told them they were compatible, and Pearl had thought she was right. But maybe she was wrong. Maybe the four of them didn't belong together after all. At least not when it came to Show Off Day.

"I wish I'd agreed to take out those solos," she murmured to a passing angelfish. "Maybe then they'd still want to try doing my song idea."

The angelfish gave her a confused look and kept swimming. Pearl blew out a sigh of shivery bubbles, then swam slowly up to the surface to take a breath.

When she returned, she looked around. Way across the cove, she could see Echo working alone, surrounded by a cloud of magical sparkles. In the other direction, Splash was doing all kinds of acrobatic flips and spins by himself. Pearl didn't see Flip, but she guessed he was working on his Show Off Day performance, too.

"Whatever that is," she muttered, trying to remember which idea Flip had liked the best. Then she shrugged. It didn't matter what Flip was going to do. If she was going solo, Pearl needed to focus on her own performance now.

Other students were also practicing all

around her. Harmony, Wiggle, and the other two dolphins from their school pod were laughing as they did flips and jumps together. The sound of Mullet, Shelly, and Finny's singing drifted along toward Pearl on the current. Another group of older students was creating an interesting light display, smiling and touching fins as they joined their magic together.

Everyone is working in a group and having fun with their friends, Pearl thought. *Everyone except us.*

She swam to a quiet corner of the cove and started to sing the song they'd been working on earlier. Then she stopped, realizing it wouldn't sound right as a solo. She would have to come up with a different idea for a song to sing on her own.

Pearl started again, trying a different melody. A reef squid that was floating nearby floated closer, waving its tentacles along with the rhythm as Pearl sang. But after only a few notes, she stopped singing and sighed. Getting ready for Show Off Day just didn't seem like much fun anymore.

At that moment Flip swam over. "Hi," he said. "What are you doing?"

"Trying to work on a song," Pearl said. "But I just keep thinking about our argument."

"Me too," Flip said. "I wish we could be a group again."

"Are you sure?" Pearl asked. "You're good at everything, remember? Maybe it will be easier to impress everyone on your own."

"Maybe." Flip shrugged. "But it won't be as much fun."

Pearl smiled. "I know what you mean." Then her smile faded as she glanced at the other two. "But Echo and Splash don't agree, so that's that."

"I don't know. I don't think we should give up on our group," Flip said. "I still think we'd be better together than apart."

"Me too," Pearl said. "But how can we convince Echo and Splash to try working together one more time? And even if we do, won't we just have the same problem all over again? We can't seem to agree on which idea to do."

"Actually, I had a great new idea about what we could do for our performance," Flip said.

Pearl groaned. "That's all we need—one more idea to argue about!"

Flip laughed. "No, listen. I think everyone will like this idea."

"Really?" Pearl eyed him doubtfully. "Because I didn't think you even cared what we did. You seemed willing to do magic when that was our plan. Then when we switched to music, you were happy to do that. And jumping and swimming, too."

"Right," Flip said. "That's my idea!"

"Huh?" Pearl stared at him, confused.

Flip grinned. "Why can't we do ALL those things?"

"All of them?" Pearl echoed, still confused. "What do you mean?"

"Nobody said we had to do *only* magic, or *only* music, or *only* jumping and swimming, right?" Flip said. "I bet we could come up with a display that uses *all* the stuff we've been learning in our classes. Then everyone will be happy, because everyone will get to do something they're good at. Plus it will make our performance really cool. It'll be like when Echo started to do magic when she was singing, remember?"

"But she wasn't supposed to do that," Pearl reminded him. "Trying to do both at the same time just distracted her and made her sound bad."

"That's because we didn't plan it that way." Flip waved his fins excitedly. "I've been thinking about it, and I know how we could do it . . ."

He talked fast, explaining his plan. The more he talked, the happier Pearl felt.

"What a great idea!" she exclaimed when he was finished. She was impressed—Flip was the only one who hadn't given up on their group. Besides that, he'd figured out the perfect way to bring all their talents and opinions together. "Your plan could really work!"

"I know!" Flip swished his tail with excitement. "Come on, let's go find the others!"

10

Show Off Day

"I'M SO NERVOUS!" ECHO EXCLAIMED, swimming in a small circle.

"Me too." Pearl shivered and glanced at the stage. A group of older students had just finished an interesting Ocean Lore demonstration about the different kinds of coral on the school reef. Now Mullet and his group were swimming into the center of the cove.

Pearl glanced around. The familiar school cove looked very different today—Show Off Day! Dolphins of all shapes and sizes were there, gathered in a big circle to watch the performances. There were so many dolphins crowded inside the school walls that Pearl could hardly see the coral behind them!

She spotted her own pod floating at the edge of the kelp forest. Her little sister, Squeak, saw her looking and waved a fin. Pearl waved back and smiled.

"I'm glad your pod could come this year," Splash said. "I bet they're excited that they finally get to see Show Off Day!"

"They are," Pearl said. "They can't wait to see our performance."

Echo reached out and touched Pearl's fin. "I can't wait, either."

Pearl smiled at her friend. She was glad that Echo and Splash had liked Flip's idea just as much as she had. The four of them had been practicing almost nonstop ever since. It felt much better being back together working as a group!

Splash did a flip and nudged them. "Look, my brother's group is about to start."

Pearl nodded and watched as Finny, Shelly, and Mullet formed a line and started to sing. "Wow," Echo whispered after a moment. "They're really good!"

"Yeah," Flip agreed. "Shelly always comes up with really neat songs."

The audience seemed to agree. There were lots of smiles during the performance. When the song ended, the entire cove erupted into a chorus of clicks, whistles, and squeaks of approval.

"They were really amazing." Pearl watched the trio swim out of the performance area.

When they passed, Splash swam up to his

brother. "You guys were great!" he said.

"Thanks," Finny said. "Good luck when you go. What are you doing, anyway?"

Splash traded a look with the rest of the group. "Um, it's sort of a surprise."

Mullet smirked. "I'll be surprised if you babies can get through a whole performance without getting so nervous you quit."

"Oh, Mullet," Shelly said with a laugh. She smiled at Pearl. "Can't you give us a hint?"

Splash glanced at the others. "Well . . . I guess you could say we're using all our different talents together."

Finny looked surprised. "What does that mean? Are you doing a song? Because I've heard Splash sing, and, well . . ."

"Not *just* a song," Echo said with a smile.

"Wait, I know," Mullet said. "You're not

trying to do more than one thing in your performance, are you?"

"Maybe." Pearl glanced nervously at her friends. "Why?"

"Because a group tried that last year." Mullet smirked. "They tried to do flips while they sang."

"Oh, I remember that!" Shelly giggled. "They kept getting mixed up and forgetting what they were supposed to do next."

"Really?" Pearl glanced at her friends. Splash and Echo looked nervous.

"I forgot about that," Splash said. "I remember watching them."

Echo nodded. "I felt really sorry for them. They didn't even finish—they just gave up and swam away after a while."

Mullet was smirking harder than ever.

"The exit's that way if you need to do the same thing," he said, waving a fin toward the break in the coral. Then he flicked his friends with his fluke. "Come on, you guys. I want to find a good spot where we can watch this disaster!"

"Oh, Mullet, you're going to make them nervous!" Shelly chided with a giggle. She brushed Pearl's side. "Break a fin, you guys!"

The three of them swam away. Pearl felt worried.

"Do you think Mullet is right?" she asked her friends. "What if it was a mistake to try to do too many things?"

"I don't know." Echo looked anxious. "Maybe we shouldn't perform at all."

Splash did a slow flip. "I don't want to quit just because of what Mullet said," he said. "But . . ."

"But what?" Flip blew bubbles in Splash's face. "Forget about Mullet, you guys. Our performance is going to be awesome!"

"But that other group—" Echo began.

"That other group wasn't us," Flip interrupted. "They probably didn't practice enough. Or maybe they didn't work together as well as we do."

"We do work together really well," Pearl murmured, touching Echo's fin.

Echo still looked nervous. But she smiled. "We're compatible."

"We're not just compatible—we're awesome," Flip declared. "And we're going to be awesome today! This is our chance to show off what we've learned, remember? *All* of it!"

That made Pearl feel much better. "Yeah!" she cheered. "We can do anything if we're doing it together. We're going to be great!"

"Really great!" Echo added.

"Really, really great!" Splash laughed. "Or at least we'll have fun, right?"

They all smiled at one another. Then Old Salty called their names. It was time to perform!

Pearl still felt a little nervous as she and her friends swam up to take a breath, then took their places in the center of the cove. She wasn't used to having so many dolphins watching her. But she tried not to think about that. Instead, she focused on her friends.

"Ready?" she whispered.

"Ready," they all whispered back.

"Let's go!" Flip added.

Pearl started to sing. Flip joined in with the harmony. Meanwhile, Echo created a light display, sending pretty sparkles and flashes out in every direction so that the lights seemed to dance along with the music. At the same time, Splash swam in a big circle around them all, doing interesting rolls and flips along the way.

After a little while, Flip stopped singing, leaving Pearl to continue on her own. She used a little magic energy to make her voice louder so everyone could hear. Swimming over to Echo, Flip touched her fin to join his magic with hers. The two of them summoned a school of beautiful blue tangs, which they directed to swim around Splash, blocking him from view. A moment later, just as Pearl reached an exciting part of her song, Splash suddenly swam up and out, bursting to the surface in a cool spinning flip. The audience gasped with amazement as he landed and the little blue fish spun around him.

Pearl smiled. So far, the show was going perfectly! Then she remembered what came next and felt nervous again. Could they do it?

As the blue tangs dispersed, Flip swam over

beside Splash. He did a backflip while Splash did a forward flip. Then they switched, and Flip did a forward flip while Splash did a backflip.

Meanwhile, Echo swam over and lined up next to Pearl. When the boys finished their flips, all four of them came together and started singing, blending their voices into Pearl's song. Splash looked a little nervous, but he kept his voice steady and didn't get confused even once! Pearl was happy about that. She'd given him extra help with his singing in yesterday's practice.

Still singing together, the whole group swam forward in unison and did a series of flips. The crowd whistled in approval.

But the performance wasn't quite over yet. When they stopped flipping, all four friends joined fins to mingle their magic. As Pearl and Flip started the last part of the song, they focused on guiding the blue tangs again, just as they'd practiced. At the same time, Splash was helping Echo create a sparkly rainbow that arced over them all. The audience gasped and burst into applause as the last few notes of the song died away.

"We did it!" Pearl whispered, rubbing her friends' fins.

"We did it." Echo smiled. "Together!"

As they swam out of the center, Pearl and her friends were mobbed by their classmates. "That was great, you guys!" Harmony exclaimed.

"Yeah," Wiggle added. "How'd you ever think of such a cool performance?"

Pearl traded a look with her friends. "It was Flip's idea," Pearl said.

"But we did it together," Flip added.

Bay swam over. "Wonderful job, all of you," the teacher said. "I'm proud to have such creative students. Especially ones who realize how all of our dolphin skills are meant to work together in harmony."

"Thanks, Bay," Echo said.

Just then Pearl's pod swam toward them. "Pearl, that was wonderful!" her mother exclaimed, rubbing her snout against Pearl's. "You and your friends really are learning a lot in school!"

"Yeah, you were the best of anyone, Pearlie!" Squeak cried, spinning around and around in excitement. "Can you guys teach me how to make those sparkles? And do those cool flips? And sing like that, too?"

Echo laughed. "You'll learn how to do all

this stuff when you go to school, Squeak," she promised.

Squeak blew out a frustrated stream of bubbles. "But I don't want to wait that long!"

Everyone laughed—even Squeak. Pearl's father rubbed Pearl's fin.

"We're proud of you, Pearl," he said.

"Thanks," Pearl said. "But I couldn't have done it without my friends, especially Flip."

Flip looked surprised. "Really?"

"Really!" Echo said with a laugh. "It was all your idea, remember?"

Splash nodded. "You're always telling us how great you are at everything," he told Flip. "I guess you were right!"

"And you're especially good at getting us to work together," Pearl added.

"I guess I am good at all that stuff." Flip

looked pleased. "It's a good thing my friends are good at everything, too!"

Pearl smiled, feeling so happy she could burst. Show Off Day was even more fun than she'd imagined. But the best part was how it had showed her that Shelly was right. Pearl and her friends worked best when they worked together.

"We're compatible," she whispered.

Flip glanced over. "What was that, Pearl?"

Pearl smiled at him. "I'll tell you later," she said. "Come on, let's go watch the rest of the Show Off Day performances together!"

Don't miss any of the

books!

#1: Pearl's Ocean
Magic

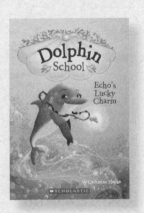

#2: Echo's Lucky
Charm

#3: Splash's Secret
Friend

If you liked Dolphin School,
check out Zoe's Rescue Zoo,
a fun series full of animals!

The cub blinked nervously at the crowd. He opened his mouth to reveal a row of white baby teeth and gave a squeaky growl. His little paws trembled and he looked very weak and frightened.

"Stand back, please!" Mr. Pinch announced as the visitors pushed forward to get a better look. "Make way for the vet."

Zoe's mom knelt down slowly next to the cub. "There, there, little one. I'm not going to hurt you," she soothed as she examined the lion's eyes, ears, teeth, tummy, and paws. The cub shrank away, snarling as fiercely as he could. Zoe's mom looked up. "You found him just in time, Uncle Horace. It looks like he hasn't eaten in weeks."

Zoe and Meep shared a worried look.

The cub seemed confused and very scared. He kept turning his head from side to side, as if he was looking for someone in the crowd. Zoe desperately wanted to explain that everyone at the Rescue Zoo was really kind and wanted to help him. But she couldn't talk to him in front of the crowd — she had to keep the animals' secret.

Zoe felt a gentle tug on her hair, and realized it was Kiki trying to get her attention.

Great-Uncle Horace was standing next to her. Leaning closer, he whispered, "My dear, this little chap needs help. Will you promise to look after him for me?"

Zoe stared at her great-uncle and then nodded. "I promise. I'll try my very best to help the cub."

The Rescue Princesses

These are no ordinary princesses—
they're Rescue Princesses!

Puppy Powers

Get your paws on the Puppy Powers series!

There's something special about the animals at Power's Pets . . . something downright magical!